I Witness

The Rumor

By Carol Gorman
Illustrated by Ed Koehler

CPH

SAINT LOUIS

To my parents, with love

Copyright © 1994 Carol Gorman
Published by Concordia Publishing House
3558 S. Jefferson Avenue, St. Louis, MO 63118-3968
Manufactured in the United States of America

Library of Congress Cataloging-in-Publication Data
Gorman, Carol.
    The rumor/Carol Gorman.
        p.   cm.—(I witness; #4)
    Summary: Samantha and Abby start a "good" rumor and discover that they need Jesus's forgiveness when the rumor becomes very damaging.
    ISBN 0-570-04631-9
    [1. Gossip—Fiction. 2. Schools—Fiction. 3. Christian life—Fiction.] I. Title. II. Series: Gorman, Carol. I witness; #4.
PZ7.G6693Ru 1994
[Fic]—dc20   93-37774

1 2 3 4 5 6 7 8 9 10   03 02 01 00 99 98 97 96 95 94

I
Witness

Series

Contents

1

The Plot Is Hatched

We had the best parties in Kimball City!" I said to my new friend, Abby Hart.

I lay back on my pillow and thought about my friends. I'd really missed them a lot since we'd moved. My family had only lived here for two weeks. I was so lonely and homesick for my friends, I'd had a stomachache almost every day.

Mom had said I could invite Abby to sleep over the second weekend. Mom knew I was missing the kids from back home, and I think she wanted me to make some new friends.

Every day after school, she had asked, "How did school go today, Samantha?" She'd looked at me anxiously, "Did you meet any nice, new friends?"

I'd said, "School's fine. Yeah, there are some nice kids in my class."

But no one like my best friend from my old school. I'd never find a friend like Elisa.

Mom was still worried though. I think it was because I hadn't brought anyone home.

Inviting a friend to sleep over was Mom's idea. I thought it would be fun. I didn't know whether Abby would become a good friend, but I hoped she would.

Abby and I had just taken baths and put on our p.j.'s and slippers. We stretched out on my bed.

"Tell me about the parties," Abby said. She lay on her side, propped up on her elbow.

I put my hands behind my head on the pillow and stared at the ceiling.

"Elisa, my best friend, always gave the best parties," I said. "Her birthday's on June 8th, so if the weather was good, we'd be outside in her backyard. She always set up the badminton net and the croquet set."

"Did she invite boys too?" Abby asked.

"No, just girls," I said. "We really had fun. She invited practically all the girls in the fourth grade!"

"Wow!" Abby said.

"Sometimes we'd go swimming or bowling," I said. "But we'd always come home and play in her yard. One thing we did every year was play the telephone game. That was fun. We always ended up laughing so hard!"

"What's the telephone game?" Abby asked.

"You don't know the telephone game?" I said. Abby shook her head no.

I sat up and pulled my knees up to my chest. "It's so much fun. Everyone sits in a circle. One girl starts by whispering a message in the ear of the person next to her. That person whispers what she hears to the next person in the circle."

"Yeah?" Abby said.

"And when everybody has heard the message, the last person says it out loud so everyone can hear." I said.

Abby frowned. "That's it?" she asked, looking disappointed. "That's the game?"

"Yeah!" I said. "Usually, the message is about someone in the circle. What's funny is that the message the last person hears is completely different from the way it started out."

"Really?" Abby said.

"Yeah," I said. "Everybody hears something just a little bit different. So when they tell the next person, it's a different message."

"I'd like to play that sometime," Abby said.

"It's kind of like a rumor," I said. "You know how rumors change when people pass them around."

"Oh," Abby said thoughtfully. "I guess I didn't know that people change what they hear."

"Oh, sure," I said. "Most of the time, they don't change it on purpose. It just happens. Like one time I heard some kids talking about a friend of my sister's. They said this girl was really, really sick. They made it sound as if she were *dying*, for pete's sake! Turned out she just had a bad sore throat."

Abby traced the star pattern on my quilt with her finger. Then she sat up.

"It'd be kind of fun to start a rumor and see if it changes," she said. "I mean, in real life."

I shrugged. "Yeah, I suppose."

Abby's face lit up. "Let's do it!" she said.

"Start a rumor?" I said.

"Yeah!" Abby said.

"I don't know," I said slowly.

This didn't feel right, but I really wanted Abby to be my friend. She was the only friend I had so far, and I didn't want her to get mad at me.

"Come on!" she said. "It'll be an *experiment*, to see if the rumor changes!"

"But I don't want anybody to get hurt," I said.

"We'll make it some *good* news about somebody!" Abby said. "That way, no one will get hurt!"

That sounded better. *Good* news about a person couldn't cause trouble, could it?

I didn't think so.

But I remembered what my Sunday school teacher, Mrs. Curtain, said once about "bearing false witness" against your neighbor. She said that meant telling lies about people or saying unkind things about them. She said that God doesn't want us to do that. And I can understand why.

But I think Mrs. Curtain meant that we shouldn't make up *bad* lies about other people.

Telling *good* things should be okay. That just made sense. I mean, God wouldn't mind if we started a good rumor, would He?

"What good rumor could we tell?" I asked Abby.

"I don't know," Abby said. "Let's think."

"And who would we tell it about?" I asked.

"Let's tell the rumor about someone who needs good things to happen," Abby said. "Like Loretta."

"Who's Loretta?" I asked.

"Loretta Smeed. She's this girl at school," Abby said. "She's in the other fifth grade, in Mrs. Wilson's class. She's kind of weird, so everybody stays away from her."

10

"She's weird?" I said.

"Yeah," Abby said. "She was in my class last year. She never says anything unless the teacher calls on her. And if you talk to her, she acts kind of suspicious or mad, like you bothered her or something. She makes a face at you and then says something mean."

"Oh," I said. "What rumor would you make up about her?"

"Something nice," Abby said. She stared at the wall with a little smile on her face. "Something kind of exciting so people will want to tell it. That's important."

Just then the door to my room was thrown open and my little sister ran in and jumped on the bed.

"Hi, Samantha! Hi, Abby!" she squealed.

"Hi, yourself, Emmy," I said. I grabbed her and tickled her silly while she shrieked with laughter. Abby sat back and watched.

My sister's real name is Emily, but I call her Emmy. Sometimes she bugs me, but tonight I was glad she interrupted. I really didn't want to start a rumor, even a nice one, and I was hoping Abby would forget what we were talking about.

"Stop it! Stop it!" squealed Emmy. I stopped tickling and sat back, laughing.

Abby sat up and leaned forward. "So what rumor are we going to start?" she asked eagerly.

Abby hadn't forgotten.

"I don't know," I said. I leaped on Emmy, pinned her on the bed and sat on her stomach. She howled with laughter. "I don't know if there are any *nice* rumors."

"Sure there are!" Abby said. "Like maybe we can say that Loretta is a great singer! And she's going to record a CD in Hollywood!"

"That wouldn't work," I said. "Everybody would want to hear the CD. Or they'd ask her to sing for them. What if she has a rotten voice?"

"Yeah, that's right," Abby said. "One time I stood next to her when we had music, and her voice sounded like a sick cat yowling."

"Get off my stomach, Samantha," Emmy said.

"Am I a wonderful, beautiful sister?" I asked her.

"No!" she said, and then screamed with laughter when I tickled her.

"Am I a *wonderful, beautiful sister?*" I asked Emmy again. "Say it!"

"Okay, okay!" she cried, still laughing. "You're a wonderful, beautiful sister!"

I got off her stomach, grinning.

"*Not!*" she shrieked.

This time I just laughed and rolled my eyes.

"I know!" Abby said, grabbing my arm to get my attention again. "Why don't we say that Loretta is related to somebody famous?"

"Like who?"

"Someone really glamorous—an actress— someone like—*Alison St. John*," she said, her eyes wide and a smile creeping across her face.

I thought about that. "What kind of relative would Loretta be?" I asked her.

"A *distant* relative," she said. "No one would believe they're close relatives. When you see Loretta, you'll know what I mean."

That sounded safe. No one in our class could possibly know a famous actress, so they couldn't ask her to find out if it were true.

"Well," I said, "I suppose it would be okay if no one ever found out it wasn't true. I mean, I can't think how it could hurt anybody."

"Great!" Abby cried.

"Samantha," said Emmy, "will you guys play Battleship with me?"

"We're planning an experiment, Emily," Abby said to her. "Maybe a little later."

Emmy looked disappointed, and I felt sorry for her. My sister was shy and hadn't made any friends here yet. I was her only friend.

But Abby was *my* only friend, other than Emmy, and I wanted her to be happy with me.

So I said to Emmy, "We'll play before we go to bed, okay?"

"Okay," she said. "Can I stay here with you guys while you plan your experiment?"

Abby looked doubtful, but I said, "Sure," before she could say anything.

"Okay," Abby said. "How do we start the rumor?"

I shrugged. "I guess we tell somebody."

Abby grinned and clapped her hands together. "This'll be so much *fun!* We'll start it tomorrow on the playground, before school."

"Okay with me," I said, smiling at her.

"I know who we can tell!" Abby said. "Hilary, Stacy, and Candy! They blab everything they hear!"

"Then let's start there," I agreed.

I was hoping we could have some fun with telling this rumor and that I could make some friends at the same time.

I was kind of excited about this little experiment, now that we'd thought of a *good* rumor to tell. At the time, though, I didn't know how easily experiments can blow up in your face.

2

Starting the Rumor

I met Abby on the playground the next morning before school. She looked as excited as I felt. I didn't know a lot of the kids yet, and I figured we'd be talking to some of them while we got the rumor going. I was a little bit scared too. Sometimes I feel as shy as Emmy, and I wonder if I'll say the right things. I wanted the kids to like me the way they did back where we used to live.

Abby had said we would get the rumor off to a good start by telling Hilary, Stacy, and Candy. I knew who they were, even though I hadn't talked much to any of them.

Hilary is a person you notice right away. Her voice is about twenty decibels louder than anyone else's, so every time she opens her mouth, it sounds as if she's talking over a loudspeaker. She also seems pretty stuck on herself. Stacy and Candy follow her around a lot and laugh at her jokes, and the three of them are always gossiping about other kids.

I figured Abby was right. They probably were the best people to start the rumor.

"There they are," Abby said in a low voice.

Abby and I leaned against the wire-mesh fence that surrounded the school. She nodded toward the big oak next to the fifth-grade classroom.

Hilary stood there talking to Stacy and Candy. I realized just then that I'd never seen one of those girls without the other two. That seemed kind of funny.

"Come on," Abby said.

I followed her to the oak.

"Hi," Abby said.

"Hi," they said back. They looked at me, then back to Abby. I suddenly felt self-conscious.

Hilary spoke up then. "I was just telling these guys what I heard about Mike Heaton."

"What?" asked Abby. She gave me a sideways glance. I'm sure she wanted me to be sure and notice they were gossiping.

"He got in a fight with Jon Horton at the mall! You should've seen them! It was really spectacular."

"You mean a fist fight?" Abby asked.

"Yeah!" Hilary said. "They were rolling around on the cement in the parking lot!"

"Wow," Abby said.

"What were they fighting about?" I asked.

"I don't know, but I bet they were fighting over Mandy Jacobs," Hilary said.

"I bet so too!" said Candy, laughing.

Stacy nodded, her eyes wide.

"And you know what?" Hilary said, giggling. "I happen to know that Mandy Jacobs can't stand either of them! She told Suzy Perkins, who told Jessie Anderson, who told me all about it!"

Abby glanced at me and managed not to smile.

Wow, I thought, talk about gossips!

"Well, we heard something really *incredible!*" Abby said, glancing over at me.

"*What?*" asked Hilary, Stacy, and Candy at the same time. They could hear gossip coming a mile away.

"You know Loretta Smeed?" Abby said.

"That grumpy girl who was in our class last year?" said Hilary. She wrinkled her nose and rolled her eyes.

"Right," Abby said. "Before I tell you, you have to promise not to tell anyone."

Hilary's eyes lit up. "*Sure!*" she said.

"*Sure!*" echoed Stacy and Candy. "We promise."

Abby leaned in closer and whispered, "Did you know she's related to Alison St. John?"

Hilary blinked. "You mean, the *actress?*" she whispered back.

"Yes!" Abby said. "Isn't that right, Samantha?"

"That's right," I said.

I felt kind of bad about standing there and telling those girls a lie, but it was too late to back out now. I'd already promised Abby I'd start this crazy rumor.

"I don't believe it!" Hilary said, her voice louder. "You made that up! That can't possibly be true!"

"It is true!" Abby said. "But don't tell anyone."

"How come?" asked Candy, leaning closer.

"Because it's just a rumor," Abby said. "So don't spread it around."

"We won't," Hilary said. "But I can hardly believe it!"

"Me either!" Candy said.

"Yeah," Stacy said, "Alison St. John is so *beautiful,* and Loretta Smeed is— well—"

"Loretta Smeed is so ugly!" Hilary said with a laugh. "She's one of the ugliest people I've ever seen!"

"Yeah," Stacy said. "How could they be related?"

Abby shrugged. "I don't know."

"Do you think they could be *cousins?*" Candy asked.

"Maybe," Abby said.

"Or aunt and niece?" suggested Stacy.

"Could be," I said.

"Look!" whispered Candy. "There's Loretta now."

We all turned to see Loretta trudging across the playground. She was thin and blond, her short hair parted on the side and hanging limp over one eye. She kind of waddled with her feet pointing out to the sides like a duck, and she stared down at the ground.

It sure was hard to imagine that she could be a relative of glamorous Alison St. John!

Hilary turned back to us. "No way," she said. "There's not any resemblance *at all!*"

Abby shrugged. "That's what I heard," she said. She looked at me. "Come on, Samantha, let's play a game of tetherball."

We said good-bye to the three girls and walked around to the other side of the school. We could hear the girls whispering together as we left.

We didn't say anything until we were far enough away that they couldn't hear us.

"*It's started!*" whispered Abby. "Our experiment will really take off now!"

"Let's write it all down in a notebook," Abby suggested. "Then we'll really be doing our experiment the way scientists do. And we can see how the rumor changes."

"Great idea," I said.

The guilt about telling the lie had left me by then. It didn't seem such a bad thing to do. After all, no one was going to get hurt. I was sure of that.

We'd walked home from school and sat on my front porch swing. Mom and Dad were still at work, and Emmy was upstairs in her room.

"I'll get a notebook from my room," I said.

"It'll be our Official Scientific Notebook!" Abby said.

"Great," I said. I dashed upstairs and grabbed an empty spiral I'd bought for school but didn't need. Coming out of my room, I noticed that Emmy's bedroom door was closed. She hardly ever closed it.

I tapped on her door and stuck my head inside. She was stretched out on her stomach on top of her bed. Her face was turned away.

"Hi, Emmy," I said. "Feeling okay?"

"No," she said, her voice muffled in her pillow.

She looked so little and skinny lying there, her hair falling off the pillow in a mess and her toothpick ankles and bony feet sticking out the bottom of her blue jeans.

"What's the matter?" I went over and sat on the edge of her bed. "Are you sick?"

She didn't move. "Everybody hates me."

"Hates you? I'm sure no one hates you," I said.

"Yes, everybody does," she said.

"*I* don't hate you," I said.

She turned over. "You don't count. You're my sister. The kids at school all have their own friends, and nobody will play with me."

I felt guilty. I'd been thinking so much about making my own friends, I'd almost forgotten about Emmy. She and I had walked to school together every day since we moved here, but when we got to the playground, I always ran off with Abby.

"Maybe you need to ask the other kids to play," I said.

Even as I said it, I knew that it was unfair to suggest something that *I* could never do. I mean, when you're shy and new in town, you stand around by yourself until someone else comes up to you and starts talking. Luckily for me, Abby walked right up to me on my first day of school. Emmy just hadn't been so lucky.

"I wish we could go back home to Kimball City," she said in a small voice.

"I know," I said. "Sometimes I do too."

I heard the front door downstairs open and close. "Samantha!" Abby called. "What's taking so long?"

"I'll be right down!" I yelled back.

Then I turned back to Emmy. "It'll be okay," I told her. "You'll make friends. You just have to give it some time. Remember, Mom told us it would be that way. She said we'd just have to wait and find some good, true friends."

"Don't go downstairs," she said, reaching up for my arm. "Stay here with me."

"But Abby's waiting," I said. "You want to come down with me? We're sitting on the front porch."

"No," she said. She let go and turned back to face the wall.

"*Samantha!*" Abby yelled again.

"Just a minute!"

"I'm going downstairs," I said to Emmy. "If you change your mind, come down. We'll be on the swing."

Emmy didn't say anything.

I ran downstairs, and Abby and I went back to the porch swing. I opened my notebook.

"Let's give our experiment a name," Abby suggested.

"Okay," I said. "Like what?"

"Hmmm," she said thoughtfully. "How about 'The Rumor Experiment'?"

"That sounds good," I said. I started to write.

"No, I have a better idea," she said. "How about 'The Good Changes Experiment'?"

"Good changes?" I said.

"Sure," she said. "I've been thinking about it, and I bet that our experiment just might change Loretta's life for the better!"

"Really?" I said. "How would that happen?"

Abby smiled. "I bet that once this rumor gets around, Loretta will be getting lots of nice attention."

"Could be," I said.

"Won't that make her feel *great?*" Abby said.

"Sure," I said. "It would make *me* happy."

"And I bet that will start changes in her life," Abby said. "*Good* changes. Maybe she'll get real popular!"

"That would be terrific!" I said.

"Yeah," she said.

So I wrote "The Good Changes Experiment" at the top of the first page.

"Okay," Abby said. "Now let's write down what we said to get the experiment going."

"Okay," I said.

I wrote:

*Rumor: Loretta Smeed is related to the gorgeous actress, Alison St. John. But this is just a rumor, so **don't tell!***

"Good," Abby said, nodding her approval. "Now we need to write down who we told the rumor to."

So I wrote:

First to hear rumor: Hilary, Stacy, and Candy (biggest gossips in the whole school!).

"Great," Abby said. "Now write the date."

I wrote:

Monday, October 15.

"Now it's an official experiment," Abby said. She grinned. "I can't wait for tomorrow to see if the rumor has changed any."

"Me either," I said. "I'll bring the Official Scientific Notebook so we can write down any changes that we hear."

"Good!" Abby said.

This really *was* exciting. I felt like a scientist of some kind, writing down all of the important information about our experiment.

I gazed out over the street and wondered: What would happen tomorrow?

3

The Rumor Changes

Emmy and I walked to school together the next morning. She hung onto my hand the whole way.

"Stay with me on the playground, okay ,Sam?"

I had promised Abby I'd meet her. We were going to walk around the playground and see if the kids were talking about Loretta. But I felt guilty about leaving Emmy again.

"I'm meeting Abby," I said. "But why don't you come with us? We're just going to wander around."

"Okay," she said, hanging her head. She sounded disappointed, but she didn't drop my hand.

"Come on," I said. "You like Abby, don't you?"

"Yeah," she said. "But I'd rather just be with you."

What she *really* needed was a friend from her own class, I thought. If only she'd make just one friend! She wouldn't need me so much, and she'd have someone to have fun with.

We found Abby leaning against the school in the sunshine.

"I'm glad you're here," she said to me. "Let's start mingling. Did you bring the O.S.N.?"

"The what?" I said.

"The O.S.N.," she said. "The Official Scientific Notebook."

I held up the red spiral. "Yup," I said. "Emmy's going to hang around with us this morning."

Abby shrugged. "Okay. Hi, Emmy."

Emmy looked up at Abby for the first time and smiled a little. "Hi," she said.

"Let's walk," Abby said to me.

We strolled over to the swings, where some kids from the fourth grade were standing. We walked near them to listen to what they were saying. They were talking about someone's birthday coming up. Maybe they hadn't heard the rumor yet.

Then we walked over to some girls playing with jacks on the sidewalk leading up to the school entrance. But they were so busy keeping track of their balls and how many jacks they had to pick up, they weren't talking about anything.

"Maybe this rumor will never get started," I said.

"I think we have to give it time," Abby said. "Let's try the girls standing over there on the map."

She was talking about the map of the United States that the fifth grade had painted on the cement a couple of years ago. All of the states were drawn in with their two-letter abbreviations.

Three girls stood together on the state of Texas.

"What class are those girls in?" I asked Abby. They definitely weren't from our class.

"They're in the other fifth grade," she said. "Heidi is the tall one, and Brandi's standing next to her. Colleen is the other girl. They're having a big conversation about something. Let's see what they're talking about. Come on."

We walked over to them.

"—But how could they be related?" Brandi said. "Alison St. John is so gorgeous!"

Abby nudged me and grinned. The rumor was spreading after all!

"What are you guys talking about?" Abby said. She sounded very innocent, and I could hardly keep from laughing.

"Didn't you hear?" Heidi said. "It's the most unbelievable thing you've ever heard! It's going around that Loretta Smeed and that beautiful actress, Alison St. John, are *relatives!* Can you believe it?"

"You're kidding!" Abby said, pretending to be shocked. "Did you know that, Samantha?" she said to me. Her eyes danced, and I knew she wanted me to play along. She was really having fun!

"No, I didn't know," I said. I decided to play my part. "Who is Loretta Smeed?"

"She's this girl in our class," Heidi said. "She's not very attractive, let's put it that way."

The other two girls grinned. "In fact, she's pretty ugly," Brandi said. "Wait till you see her."

Abby pointed to Emmy and me and turned to the three girls. "This is Samantha Crowley and her sister Emily," she said. "They just moved here a couple of weeks ago."

"Hi," I said to them.

"Hi," they said to Emmy and me.

Emmy smiled shyly and clung to my hand.

"Anyway," Heidi said, "I heard that Loretta doesn't want it to get around that she's related to Alison St. John."

Abby looked at me and grinned. This was our first twist in the story: Loretta didn't want it to get around.

"Why?" I asked. "If I were related to Alison St. John, I'd want everybody to know!"

"Me too," said Colleen, giggling. "I'd be telling *everybody!*"

"Me too," chimed in Brandi.

"This is just too weird," Heidi said. She shook her head. "It doesn't make sense."

"Maybe Loretta's embarrassed to tell anyone," Brandi suggested, "because she knows that everyone would talk about how beautiful Alison is and how ugly *she* is! I mean, it's pretty hard not to compare the way they both look!"

"Yeah," Colleen said. "It's the first thing *I* thought about!"

"Maybe," said Heidi. "I wonder what she'd say if we asked her about it?"

My stomach clenched up suddenly. *Oh, no!* I thought. What if the kids ask her about the rumor? Wouldn't Loretta be upset that kids were telling wild stories about her? I looked over at Abby. She looked worried too.

"Oh, I don't think that would be a good idea," Abby said quickly. "I mean, you said yourself that Loretta doesn't want the story getting around."

"Yeah," said Colleen. "I don't think we should say anything to Loretta about it. Besides, she gets mad all the time at little things. Think how she'd act if she knew that all the kids know about her and Alison St. John!" Heidi giggled. "Boy, would she be mad!"

"And embarrassed, too, I bet," Colleen said.

29

"We won't say anything to her about it," Brandi said. "But maybe somebody else around here knows why Loretta is so afraid someone will find out her secret."

"Yeah," Heidi said. "Let's ask around. Maybe somebody knows the whole story."

"Good idea," Abby said. I knew she was fanning the flames so the rumor would spread faster. "Let us know what you find out. And we'll tell you if we hear anything."

"Good," Heidi agreed.

The bell rang, and we all started walking toward the school door. Emmy squeezed my hand harder."

Don't worry," I whispered to her. "It'll be okay once you get to know more kids." I turned to Abby. "I'm going to walk with Emmy."

Abby nodded. She leaned closer and whispered, "At recess, we'll write in the O.S.N."

"Okay," I said.

"Will you walk me to my room?" Emmy asked me softly. "I mean, all the way down and stay there till I get to my desk?"

"Sure," I said. We came to the school entrance and walked in with lots of other kids.

"I'm scared," she whispered.

"But you've been here for almost two weeks now," I said. "You don't have anything to be worried about. The kids are nice, aren't they?"

"The kids hate me," she whispered. "They really, really do."

"How could they hate a nice kid like you?" I said.

"They all have their own friends," she said. "They don't need any more. I'm just a leftover."

We stopped at her locker and she took off her jacket. There was a red sweater already in there.

"Who's your locker partner?" I asked her.

"Her name's Hannah," Emmy said. "She sits on the other side of the room. She won't talk to me."

"Did you talk to her?" I asked her.

There was a moment of silence. "No."

"Well," I said. "All you have to say is hi. Why don't you try it? Just say hi sometime today."

Emmy didn't respond. "Think you can do that?" I asked. "Then tell me about how it went after school today."

"Okay," Emmy said. She looked at the floor and I wondered if she really would say hi to Hannah.

We walked to the second grade classroom and stopped in the doorway. Kids in her class passed by without saying "hi" to her, without even noticing she was there. I could see why she called herself an "extra." It looked as if they didn't care whether she was there or not.

Emmy looked so lonely.

Tears came to the corners of her eyes, and she blinked quickly, trying to make them stay where they were. One tear escaped, though, and trickled down her cheek.

I felt an ache in my chest. Emmy used to be such a happy kid. She loved school. Now she was so quiet and sad. I felt like giving her a big, long hug, but I knew she'd lose it if I did that. I didn't want her to be any more embarrassed than she already was.

"Which one's Hannah?" I whispered to her.

"She's sitting over by the pencil sharpener," Emmy whispered.

I looked and saw a small girl with blond hair sitting at her seat. She stared at the top of the desk.

"Okay," I said. "Now's a good time. Go say hi. Then tell me about it later."

Emmy bit her lower lip. "I don't think I can," she said quietly.

"Sure, you can," I said. "Just the way you did back home with your old friends."

I put a hand on her shoulder. "See you after school."

She looked up at me. "Bye," she whispered.

I watched as she slowly walked into the room toward Hannah. When she was about halfway there, she suddenly turned and walked back to her own desk and sat down. She looked over at me with tears in her eyes and mouthed the words *I can't.*

Poor Emmy. I waved to her and made myself smile. Then I walked down the hall to my own classroom.

"This is so *exciting!*" Abby said. "Our experiment is really taking off!"

It was morning recess and we sat under a big elm at the edge of the playground.

"It sure is," I said.

I opened our official notebook and turned to the second page. I wrote:

October 16

"Now we need to write how the rumor has changed," Abby said.

I wrote:

Changes in experimental rumor: Loretta doesn't want anyone to know that she is related to Alison St. John!

"Good!" said Abby. "Now write down what Brandi said."

"What?"

"You know," Abby said. "About Loretta being embarrassed—"

"Oh, yeah." I thought a minute about how I'd write it. Then I wrote:

Brandi thinks maybe Loretta is embarrassed because everyone will say she's much uglier than beautiful Alison St. John.

"Yes," Abby said. "I think we're being very scientific about this Good Changes Experiment."

"We're going to have to be careful, though," I said.

"Of what?"

"Well, those girls were ready to go and ask Loretta about the rumor," I said.

Abby grinned. "But I talked them out of it."

"We were lucky to be standing there!" I said. "A lot of people will hear this rumor. The next time someone wants to ask Loretta about it, we might not be there to talk them out of it."

"That's true," Abby said.

"We didn't think of that," I said, "when we decided to start this rumor."

"It'll be okay," Abby said. "Don't worry."

But I *was* worried. I hoped this Good Changes Experiment really made good changes and not bad.

4

Another Twist

So did you say hi to Hannah?" I asked Emmy on the way home from school that day.

We had already walked a block, and she hadn't said a word. She seemed sad as usual.

"I started to," she said. "Just like you said. I started walking over to her, but then she looked at me."

"Yeah?" I said. "She looked at you?"

"Uh-huh," she said. "And then she looked away."

"Okay," I said. "Then what?"

"*She looked away!*" Emmy cried. "*She didn't want to talk to me!*"

"How could you know that?" I asked her.

"She looked at the wall so she wouldn't have to talk to me," Emmy explained. "It's what I would do if I didn't want to talk to somebody."

"Maybe there was a fly on the wall," I said. "And she looked over at it."

Emmy rolled her eyes. "Give me a break," she said. "I could tell she didn't want to talk to me."

"Did you talk to anyone today?" I asked.

"The teacher called on me twice," she said. "And I answered the questions right."

"Good for you!" I said.

We'd come to the corner, so we stopped and looked for traffic. I didn't see any cars, but I did see Loretta Smeed. She was about a half-block ahead of us around the corner.

I took Emmy's hand, and we crossed the street while I watched Loretta. She had a funny walk. Her feet pointed out and her head swung from side-to-side. Her hair swung, too, covering her eyes every time she stepped onto her left foot. She looked pretty funny, but I felt sorry for her. I hoped the rumor would really make some good changes for her.

"Hey, Loretta!" a voice yelled.

I looked ahead to see two girls walking in front of her. They had turned and noticed her.

"Hurry up, and we'll wait!" they called out. They were smiling at her as if they liked Loretta a lot. I wondered if they'd heard the rumor about Loretta.

Loretta's head went up as she looked at them. But she didn't hurry. In fact, she slowed down just a little.

"Looks like Loretta's getting kind of popular," I said. "It sure would be nice if she made some friends."

"Yeah," Emmy said.

The girls walked back toward Loretta and stopped when they reached her. They talked a moment; then all three of them continued walking down the street, the other two girls doing most of the talking on either side of Loretta.

"Maybe I'll say hi tomorrow," Emmy said.

"What?" I wasn't paying attention to her.

"Hannah," Emmy said. "Maybe I'll say hi to her tomorrow. *Maybe*."

I looked at Emmy. "Really?" I said. "Terrific! It won't be hard. Just say hi the way you did to your old friends back home."

"I'll tell you about it," she said.

I grinned. "Yeah, I want to hear about it."

My mom and dad are busy people. They both work hard, and when they get home, they don't have a lot of time to sit down and talk. They're usually busy with getting supper and doing chores around the house.

So I hadn't told them what Abby and I were doing with the Good Changes Experiment. And I hadn't told them that Emmy was so unhappy. Emmy and I are really close, and she usually comes to me when she's upset. I knew she hadn't told Mom or Dad about how unhappy she was.

"How was your day?" Mom asked me.

She had changed into her jeans and was shuffling around the kitchen getting supper ready. She and Dad trade off nights to cook. I like Dad's nights better, because Mom's kind of a lousy cook. I'd never tell her that, though. She loves to cook and experiments a lot on us. We're her guinea pigs.

"My day was okay," I said. "What are we having for supper?

"It's something special," Mom said. "I made it up."

Uh-oh, I thought. "What's it called?" I asked her.

"Lentil-Zucchini Surprise," Mom said.

Just what I thought, another weird dish.

"What's the surprise?" I asked.

Mom smiled slyly. "Well, it wouldn't be a surprise if I told you, now would it?"

I decided to make myself a peanut butter and jelly sandwich soon after supper. I knew I wouldn't

39

be eating much of Mom's dinner, and I'd be hungry.

I watched Mom work. She started humming to herself.

I kind of wanted to tell her about Abby's and my experiment. But I didn't know how she would react. Then I thought of something. Maybe I could ask her about it without telling her exactly what we were doing.

Mom was chopping some zucchini on a cutting board. I stood next to her and leaned my elbows on the kitchen counter.

"Do you like science?" I asked her.

She stopped humming long enough to ask, "You mean, did I like it when I was a student?"

"Well, I mean, just in general," I said.

"Sure," she said. "If it weren't for science, we wouldn't have medicine or doctors or astronauts . . ." She paused. "Of course, it was God who provided that doctors and astronauts and every other scientist would have a wonderful universe to study and learn from."

"Yeah," I said. "But what about experiments? Do you think it's a good idea to experiment with different things?"

Mom raised one eyebrow. "Is this a comment about my Lentil-Zucchini Surprise?"

"No," I said. "I mean, do you think it's good to make scientific experiments where you study things and write down everything that happens? And then you study it after it's all over and decide whether it was a good experiment or not?"

"Sure," she said.

"Good," I said. "I'm glad you think so. Because I do too."

She stopped chopping. "Did I miss something?" she asked.

"Nope," I said. "Thanks, Mom." She looked kind of puzzled, and I turned to leave. I heard her start humming again as I pushed through the swinging kitchen door.

I was glad Mom felt that way about experiments. Maybe she wouldn't mind that Abby and I were in the middle of one.

When Emmy and I got to school the next morning, we saw Loretta right away. She was nearly surrounded with kids, mostly girls, who were smiling and talking to her.

Zowee! I thought. Because of our experiment, it looked as if Loretta had gone from a girl everybody ignored to the most popular girl in the school!

When we got a little closer, I could see the expression on her face. She looked suspicious. I bet she wondered why, the last couple of days, other kids wanted to be around her.

"Wow, look at that," Emmy said softly to me.

"Looks like our experiment really *has* started some good changes!" I said. "This is exciting!"

Then I saw Abby. She stood back from Loretta and the rest of the kids. She was looking and me and grinning.

I smiled back. She pointed to Loretta, started to laugh, and covered her mouth with her hand.

I nodded.

"Come on," I said to Emmy. "Let's go talk to Abby."

"Isn't it great?" Abby said when we were standing next to her. "Look at all the friends she has now!"

"Yeah," I said.

But, for some reason, I didn't feel all that happy about it. Maybe it was because the kids were acting like Loretta's friends just because they thought Loretta was related to a famous actress. This whole thing was happening because of a lie.

It just didn't feel right. Please, God, I prayed. Don't let Loretta get hurt in all this.

I looked up then to see Heidi, Brandi, and Colleen walking quickly toward us.

"Look who's coming," I whispered to Abby.

Heidi smiled as they got closer. "Look at who's so popular today!" she said.

"We were just talking about Loretta," Abby said. "It's kind of fun to see her with all those kids."

"Well, I'm sure they're all just dying to know about the feud!" Brandi said.

"Feud?" Abby said. "What feud?"

Heidi's eyes got big. "Haven't you heard?"

"Heard what?" Abby asked, looking excited.

We knew we were about to hear another twist to the rumor.

"Loretta's family is feuding with Alison St. John and her family!" Heidi said. "I'm surprised you haven't heard! It's all over school!"

"Why are they feuding?" I asked.

Heidi shrugged. "Who knows?"

"Where did you hear about the feud?" Abby asked her.

"Oh, I don't know," Heidi said. "Somebody told me, I guess. Maybe it was Stacy. No, I bet it was Hilary."

"Uh-huh," Abby said, nodding. She glanced at me, trying not to smile. She was really getting a kick out of this.

"But the feud must be the reason why Loretta doesn't want anyone to know that she's Alison St. John's niece!" Colleen said.

"Wait a minute," I said. "Loretta is Alison St. John's *niece*?"

Another twist!

Abby started to laugh and slapped a hand over her mouth.

"Yeah," said Brandi. "I bet Loretta's family hates Alison's family!"

"Yeah," Heidi agreed. "If you feud with somebody, you usually hate 'em too."

"But I wonder why Loretta would be feuding with her own aunt?" Abby said.

"Maybe Loretta's family is jealous that Alison hit it big in show business!" Brandi said.

"Yeah," said Heidi, "and all of the good-looking genes ended up on Alison's side of the family."

Everybody laughed.

"Alison got everything!" Colleen said. "And Loretta got nothing! She's one of the ugliest people I've ever seen!"

I looked over at Loretta, who was still surrounded with kids. I wondered if anyone would

44

ask her about the feud with her aunt. She wouldn't have any idea what they were talking about!

"I hope nobody asks her about the feud," I said to the girls. "She'd be pretty upset."

"Oh, yeah!" Abby said, realizing what I meant. "I hope nobody says anything to her."

"Well, *I* sure want to know!" Heidi said. "And I think she should tell us! We're all dying to know!"

"It's none of our business!" I said. Oh, please, God, I prayed, don't let anyone ask Loretta about the rumor!

I knew for sure now that Abby and I had made a mistake starting this rumor. It was really getting out of control!

We had wanted to *help* Loretta with our experiment, but it looked as if it might just do the opposite. How were we going to get out of this?

5

Disaster!

I said hi to Hannah today," Emmy said.

We were walking home from school. We'd hardly said a word to each other until now. I'd been thinking about Loretta and the rumor that was running like crazy around the school. I kept asking God to fix it so that Loretta wouldn't hear the rumor.

I didn't know how God would feel about my asking Him to fix it. I hoped He wouldn't be mad at me for starting the rumor in the first place. But He had to know Abby and I had done it so that *good* things could happen.

The more the rumor changed, the juicier the story got, and that's what really scared me. The juicier the story, the more people would talk about it. I was so afraid someone would tell Loretta what was going around about her. And *that* would be a DISASTER!

"Did you hear me?" Emmy said. "I said hi to Hannah today."

My mind snapped to attention. "Oh, you did!" I said. "That's great! What did *she* say?"

"She said hi too," Emmy said. "She even smiled at me."

"Good!" I said. "You're off to a good start."

"Yeah," Emmy said. "She invited me to come over to her house this weekend."

"That's wonderful, Emmy," I said. "It's really nice to have a friend." In spite of feeling kind of sick about the rumor, I was awfully glad Emmy had found a friend. I sure was glad I'd found Abby, and I wanted Emmy to feel as happy here as I did.

"Yeah," Emmy said. "Maybe living here won't be so bad after all."

I was glad Emmy was feeling happier. Now, I thought, I could really concentrate on figuring out what to do about the rumor.

I called Abby on the phone after supper that night.

"Hi, Abby," I said. "It's me: Samantha."

"Hi!" she said. She lowered her voice. "I've been waiting to hear from you! Did you write in the O.S.N.?"

"Yeah," I said. "But I'm getting worried."

"Worried?" she said. "Why?"

"I think someone's going to tell Loretta the rumor."

"Oh, don't worry about it," Abby said.

"I think we *should* worry about it!" I said. "What will she think? This experiment was supposed to make *good* things happen! But I think she'll be really upset when she hears it!"

"My mom says, 'Don't borrow trouble,' " Abby said. "That means don't get upset over something that hasn't happened yet."

"But you know it'll happen," I said. "Sooner or later, somebody's going to ask Loretta about her relative, the famous actress. Somebody will get so curious they just can't stand not knowing, and they'll *ask* her!"

"Maybe the rumor will just fizzle and die," Abby said. "Maybe everybody will forget about it."

"Not unless something completely different happens that gets their attention," I said. "And I sure don't know what *that* could be!"

There was a pause. "You mean, like *another* rumor?" she said finally. That's it! That's going to solve our problem!"

"Another rumor?"

"We could start another rumor!" Abby said enthusiastically. "We can get the kids to believe anything we want!"

"No way!" I said. "I've had enough of lies and rumors!"

"But it could work!" Abby said.

"I'm not even going to listen to you," I said.

"No, listen!" Abby said. "We could say that—"

"I'm going to hang up," I said. "I don't want to hear about any more experiments."

"We could say that Loretta is adopted!" Abby said. "That's why she doesn't look anything like Alison. Then the kids would lose interest because Loretta wouldn't really be related to Alison."

"Bye, Abby," I said. Then I hung up.

"Hi, Emily!"

Hannah and another girl ran over to meet Emmy when we arrived at school the next morning.

Emmy grinned. "Hi, Hannah. Hi, Margie," she said.

"Want to play hopscotch with us?" Hannah asked.

"Yeah," Emmy said. She looked up at me, looking happier than I'd seen her in three weeks. "Bye, Sam!"

"Bye, Emmy," I said. "See you after school."

Emmy ran off, giggling, with the girls. Three more girls joined them on the sidewalk next to the school building. They drew some lines with chalk and started playing right away.

Seeing Emmy so happy made me feel great. Now maybe she would spend less time thinking about our old home and be happy again. I really wanted Emmy to be her old self, and I had a feeling that these new friends would turn her back into the Emmy I've always known.

Just then I spotted Abby standing with Heidi, Brandi, Colleen, Candy, and Stacy. Hilary was there too. Abby looked worried and waved frantically.

My heart started thumping hard as I ran over. *What change had the rumor taken this time?*

"Alison St. John just *left* her!" Heidi was saying. "Can you believe that?"

"That's terrible!" said Brandi. "And I always liked watching her movies! Well, I'm sure not going to bother with Alison St. John movies *now.*"

"What's going on?" I asked Abby.

"There's a new twist," Abby whispered.

"What?" I said.

Stacy turned to me. "You haven't *heard?*"

"Haven't heard what?" I asked, my stomach twisting too, into a hard knot. I didn't want to hear this.

"Tell Samantha what you heard, Heidi," Stacy said.

Heidi turned to me, her face bright with excitement. "She's her *daughter!*" Heidi said.

"Who's whose daughter?" I said, but I was afraid I knew what Heidi meant.

"*Loretta is Alison St. John's daughter!*" Heidi said.

"Is that incredible, or what?" said Brandi. She grinned and her eyes shone.

"That can't be true!" I said. How would I ever convince them that this new horrible twist was wrong?

"That's what I told them!" Abby said. She looked really scared.

"It's true!" Hilary said. "That's why Loretta looks so lonely and sad all the time."

"Yeah," Stacy said. "She's missing her mother."

"Her mother who would rather live in Hollywood as a famous star than live here with ugly Loretta!" Hilary said.

"That's why Loretta is living with her aunt!" said Brandi. "And that's why the two families are fighting. They think Alison is terrible!"

"Well, she *is* terrible!" Colleen said. "What kind of a mother would leave her own daughter? Even if she could live in Hollywood as a famous movie star. She should have Loretta with her!"

"Maybe Alison is ashamed to be the mother of such an unattractive girl!" said Brandi.

Stacy nodded. "You might be right about that."

"Where did you guys hear this terrible rumor?" Abby asked.

"I heard it from Brandi," said Colleen.

"I heard it from Heidi," said Brandi.

"I heard it from Hilary," said Heidi.

"And who told all of this to you?" I asked Hilary.

"*Everybody* knows it!" said Hilary. "The whole school, practically!"

I looked at Abby and she looked straight back at me. We were both feeling awful. I had a pain in my stomach, and I was getting a headache. Please, God, I prayed. I have to stop this, but I don't know how. Help me know what to say.

"Poor Loretta!" said Colleen. "I feel so sorry for her."

"I think we should do something to cheer her up," Brandi said.

"Yeah," said Stacy. "What should we do? Give her a party or something? That might be a good idea! Give her a party and show her how much we all like her!"

"I think," I said carefully, "the best thing we can do for Loretta is to forget everything we've heard."

"Right," said Abby. "Good idea."

"This is all just a *rumor*," I reminded them. "We don't even know that it's true."

"Oh, it's true, all right," Hilary said.

"How could you know that?" I asked her.

"I can see a resemblance between the two of them," Hilary said.

My mouth must have dropped wide open. "Alison St. John and *Loretta?*" I said. "You're kidding!"

"I think they look alike too," said Brandi.

"Look carefully at Loretta around her eyes," said Colleen.

"Yeah, you'll see that they both have the same eyes," Stacy said.

"Their eyes aren't *anything* alike!" Abby said. "Except they're blue!"

"Well, that's something!" said Heidi.

I looked around the group of girls. "There are eight of us standing here," I said to Heidi. "Three of us have blue eyes, but none of us is related to Alison St. John!"

Heidi screwed up her face. "Huh?" she said.

"This is just a *rumor!*" I said. "You can't believe it! It's so ridiculous! A few days ago, you were all saying that Loretta and Alison couldn't be related because they didn't look anything alike!"

"Well," said Heidi, "I hadn't looked very hard at Loretta. Now I have. They look similar."

"This just isn't true!" I said.

"Well, there's one easy way to find out," said Heidi.

"Yeah," said Stacy. "Let's ask Loretta!"

"Yeah!" the girls echoed. "Let's ask her! That's the fast way to find out once and for all."

"You can't do that!" said Abby.

This was just horrible! It was like a terrible nightmare, and I couldn't wake up!

"No, you can't do that," I said. *Please, God, what can I say to change their minds?* "What if it's true? Wouldn't it be bad enough for Loretta to have a mother who didn't care about her? If everybody knew about it, she'd feel even worse!"

"That's true!" Abby said. "The worst thing you could do would be to ask Loretta about it. She'd be so embarrassed, she'd just want to *die*."

"I don't know about that," Heidi said. "Maybe she'd be glad her secret's out. Then she could just relax and not have to hide it anymore."

"Maybe she'll tell us about Alison!" said Colleen.

"I wonder if Loretta ever sees her?" said Heidi.

"I bet Alison sends Loretta expensive Christmas presents," Hilary said.

"Yeah," said Brandi. "I bet she does too, because she feels guilty about dumping her daughter on her sister to raise."

Hilary nodded. "I bet Alison sends Loretta wonderful, expensive stuff!"

"Well," said Heidi, "she sure isn't sending Loretta clothes! That's for sure!"

"Yeah, Loretta's clothes are terrible," said Stacy.

"Maybe Loretta keeps the clothes that Alison sends her in her closet," suggested Colleen. "Because she's mad at her mom for running off to Hollywood."

"Maybe," said Heidi.

Hilary's eyes narrowed. "I'd sure like to get a look in her closet. Then we'd know for sure!"

"Yeah!" said Heidi. "Maybe we can get ourselves invited to her house. Then we wouldn't have to come right out and ask her about Alison St. John! We'd know just by seeing the beautiful clothes in her closet!"

Oh, this was just terrible! It kept getting worse and worse!

"I don't think—" I said.

"No, this is a good idea," said Heidi. "Let's ask her if we can come over to her house tomorrow!"

"Yeah," said Hilary. "You and I will do it, Heidi. We'll just walk up to Loretta and tell her we want to play after school, and we'll ask if we can go to her house!"

"No, please don't," said Abby.

"What's it to you?" said Hilary, looking at Abby.

"I don't want to see Loretta get hurt," Abby said.

"She won't get hurt," said Heidi. "We just want to look in her closet. She won't even know what we're doing."

"I want to know what's in there," said Hilary. "And I'm going to find out!"

Abby turned to look at me. I knew she was thinking, *What can we do?*

I sure didn't know.

Why wouldn't God fix things for me? This was such a mess!

This rotten experiment of ours was blowing up in our faces.

Ka-BOOM!

6

Loretta's Closet

We've got to get ourselves invited to Loretta's house too! We've got to be there when Hilary and those guys ask to see her room!" Abby said to me at lunchtime.

We sat together at the end of one of the long lunch tables in the gym. The janitors always drag out the tables from under the stage at about 11:30 and set them up on the polished wood floor.

For once, I agreed with Abby. We had better go to Loretta's house with Hilary and Heidi to make sure that they didn't spill the beans about Loretta being Alison St. John's daughter.

I could see Hilary and Heidi sitting with their heads together at a table across the room. I was sure they were plotting how to get invited to Loretta's house.

Abby saw them too. "Look at them," she said. "Two girls who could make Loretta miserable this afternoon."

I looked back at Abby. "You might as well be pointing at us, Abby," I said. "Two girls who could make Loretta miserable today."

"How are we going to get ourselves invited?" I asked Abby.

"Simple," Abby said. "We'll just tell the two H's that we want to come too."

"The two H's?" I said.

"Hilary and Heidi," Abby said.

"Oh, yeah," I said. "Okay."

"Let's tell them right after lunch," Abby said.

"Good idea," I said.

Even though we were having pizza for lunch, I didn't have much of an appetite. I was too worried about what was going to happen this afternoon.

As soon as we were all dismissed to go outside, Abby and I ran to find Hilary and Heidi.

We found them by the flagpole.

"We're waiting for Loretta to come outside," Heidi said.

"We want to come with you to her house," Abby said.

"I thought you guys didn't think it was a good idea," said Hilary.

"We changed our minds," I said.

"Okay," Heidi said. "Look, there she is."

Loretta was wearing a pair of old jeans, a faded blouse, and clunky brown shoes. She walked slowly around the side of the school.

Hilary waved. "Oh, Loretta!" she sang out with a big smile. I felt like telling Hilary that she didn't fool anyone with that phony smile of hers. But there wasn't time. Loretta was looking our way.

Hilary lowered her voice. "Come on," she said.

We walked over to Loretta. She took a step back as if she were afraid of us or something.

"Hi, Loretta!" said Heidi.

"Good to see you, Loretta," Hilary said with that fake smile.

Abby and I said hi.

Loretta didn't answer. She just watched us with a suspicious look on her face.

"What's new?" Heidi asked her.

"Nothing," she said. Her eyes darted around at our faces.

"We were just talking about you!" said Hilary, her voice gooey and sweet. "We just realized that we've never even been to your house!"

I rolled my eyes. I couldn't help it. This would never get an invitation to Loretta's.

"I don't even know where you live," said Heidi.

Loretta threw her head back and to the side to get the hair out of her eyes. It fell limply back where it had been.

"I live on Mercy Lane," she said softly.

"Oh, I know where that is," Abby said. "Near the A&P grocery store."

"Yeah," Loretta said.

"You want to get together with us after school?" Hilary asked her.

Loretta's eyes darted around at our faces again.

"What were you going to do?" she asked us. She looked kind of scared.

"Oh, just hang around," said Hilary. "Why don't we come to your house?"

"My house?" Loretta said.

"Sure!" Hilary said. "I'm tired of my house and Heidi's house. I want to go to your house for a change."

"Yeah," said Heidi.

"That'd be fun," I said.

There was a long pause. Then she said, "Okay." She even smiled a little.

I felt terrible, just terrible. Loretta's smile didn't make me feel any better. In fact, seeing her smile made me feel even more guilty. We didn't want to be her friends. Hilary and Heidi wanted to look in her closet at all the clothes they thought her famous mother had sent her. Abby and I wanted to go to try and keep the two H's from telling her about the rumor.

What a mess!

I'm so sorry, God, for the mess I got myself into! Why, oh why, did I let Abby talk me into this rumor thing in the first place?

"Great!" said Hilary. "We'll walk home with you then."

"Okay," Loretta said.

"We'll meet you here by the flagpole," Hilary said.

"Okay."

Hilary and Heidi looked at each other, victory in their eyes. They'd get a chance to see Loretta's closet and all those beautiful clothes from Hollywood.

I just hoped that Abby and I could keep them from telling Loretta about the horrible rumor that we had started.

Abby and I got to the flagpole first after school. Then Hilary and Heidi arrived. We stood around nervously waiting for Loretta. She was late.

"Where's Loretta?" Hilary asked.

"I don't know," Heidi said. "She scooted out of the classroom as soon as our teacher let us go."

"Do you think she ran home so she wouldn't have to see us?" Hilary asked.

"No," I said. "I think I saw her go into the girls' bathroom."

"She's nervous!" Hilary said, grinning. "She's nervous that we're coming home with her because we're popular and she's not."

What a rotten thing for Hilary to say. I mean, she was probably right, but it was rotten, anyway, to say it. And especially to feel so happy about it.

"Shh!" Abby whispered. "Here she comes."

Loretta loped toward us from the school door. She stopped a short distance away.

"Hi," she said softly.

"Hi, Loretta," Hilary cooed at her.

"Let's go," Abby said.

Loretta nodded, and we started walking. We hardly talked the whole way to her house. I saw her take sideways glances at each of us during our walk. I suppose she was trying to figure out why we wanted to come home with her.

She seemed pretty happy, though, with us surrounding her all the way home.

Poor Loretta. If she only knew what Abby and I had done to her!

"This is it," Loretta said, turning up the front walk to an old two-story house. The house's white paint was peeling in spots, but there was a big oak tree in the front yard, and the bronze chrysanthemums growing next to the wide front porch looked pretty. It was a nice house, I guess, but it sure wasn't the kind of house you'd expect the daughter of a famous movie star to live in.

Of course, Loretta *wasn't* the daughter of a famous movie star. But Hilary and Heidi thought she was, so I figured they were thinking it was too bad that Loretta had to live in this plain old house instead of her mother's mansion in Hollywood.

Loretta led us up the porch steps and through the front door.

We walked into the hallway. From there we could see the living room to the right and the dining room to the left. A flight of stairs climbed into the darkness above us.

Heavy curtains in the living room shut out the sunshine. The furniture was large and plain, and built of heavy, dark wood.

I didn't like the feeling I had in Loretta's house. It was too dark, too quiet and—well, kind of sad.

But maybe it wasn't the house that was sad. I was feeling sad for Loretta because of our terrible rumor.

"Where's your aun—I mean, your mother?" asked Heidi. She corrected herself when Hilary jabbed her hard in the ribs.

"She's at work," Loretta said, glancing back and forth between Heidi and Hilary.

"Do you have brothers or sisters?" I asked her.

"No," she said. "It's just me."

"Can we see your room?" Hilary asked.

Loretta frowned. "How come?"

"We just want to see it," said Heidi. "Wouldn't you want to see our rooms?"

Loretta shrugged.

"Okay," she said. "It's upstairs."

She started up the steps and we followed behind. She led us to a room at the back of the house.

Her headboard stood next to the back wall. Her bed, like the furniture downstairs, was big, old, and made of dark wood. A chest of drawers standing as high as my nose stood at a side wall.

The only furniture in the room that wasn't made of wood was a banged-up metal office desk that sat hunched next to her closet door.

Hilary and Heidi looked around, disappointment written on their faces. I'm sure they expected to see Loretta's whole room filled with expensive gifts from her millionaire mother.

Hilary's eyes went to Loretta's closet door. She walked over and placed her hand on the doorknob.

"Is this your closet?" Hilary asked. She tried to sound innocent, but she didn't pull it off very well. Her eyes were too bright and her voice was too excited.

I could hear Heidi draw in a breath, waiting for Hilary to open it so she could see the expensive clothes inside.

"Yeah," said Loretta. "It's not very big."

"Oh, but it's *what's inside* that counts!" Hilary said with an excited shriek of a laugh.

"OPEN IT!" Heidi squealed, no longer trying to control herself.

Hilary threw the door open and we all stepped forward and looked at the clothes hanging there.

The old, drab clothes that we'd seen Loretta wear every day to school.

No one said anything for a moment.

Then Hilary made a little noise in her nose that sounded like the last rush of air escaping from a released balloon.

Uh-oh, I thought. *Here it comes!*

"What—?" Hilary started to say.

"Uh, nice room, Loretta!" Abby said quickly in a voice that was much too loud. "Let's go downstairs and play a game or something."

"But—y-your clothes—" Heidi stammered.

"What about my clothes?" Loretta said. The suspicious look was back on her face.

"They're *great* clothes!" Abby said. She turned to me. "Right, Samantha?"

"*I* think so," I said.

"Stylish, up-to-date, everything a girl could want!" Abby said loudly.

Boy, was she overdoing it. We'd better get off this clothes topic real fast!

"I like the idea of going downstairs for a game," I said, edging toward the door.

"But what about your clothes?" Hilary cried.

"What do you mean?" Loretta said. She was starting to look mad.

"Where are the expensive things?" Hilary demanded. "The things your *mother* gave you?"

"Come on!" Abby yelled frantically. "Everybody downstairs!"

"Yeah!" I said. "Come on! Let's play Monopoly or something!"

Loretta turned to Abby and me and hollered, "Shut up!" Then she looked back at Hilary. "What are you talking about?"

"Hasn't your crummy mother sent you any clothes from Hollywood?" Hilary asked angrily.

"What!" Loretta said.

"Nothing!" Abby said. "Hilary's having an attack of some kind! Ignore her."

"Come on, you guys!" I begged. "Let's go—"

"I said, *SHUT UP!*" Loretta yelled at us even louder than before.

That was when I knew it would all come apart. Loretta was now going to hear the rumor. The whole, big, ugly rumor.

"I want to know about these clothes," Hilary whined.

"Know *what?*" Loretta asked. "What are you talking about?"

"Hasn't Alison St. John sent you some nice clothes from Hollywood?" Hilary demanded. *"It's the least she can do after she ran off and gave you to her sister to raise!"*

Loretta stopped and stared at Hilary with her mouth hanging wide open.

"Everybody knows about it," Heidi said in a gentler voice. "We know that Alison St. John is your mother and that she abandoned you and that you're being raised by your aunt. We're sorry that you have to live this way." She raised her hands and gestured to the room around us.

"Don't get mad at *us!*" Hilary said. "We feel sorry for you!"

Loretta continued to stare at Hilary and Heidi. Then her eyes filled up with tears and she ran out of the room. Her feet clomped all the way down the hall and down the wooden stairs. The front door opened and slammed shut.

"She ran away," Hilary said, her eyes big.

"Gee, I wonder why," Abby said sarcastically.

And that was that. That's how our Good Feelings Experiment ended. With Hilary and Heidi spilling the beans and Loretta crying and running out of her house.

Some good feelings! Some scientific experiment!

All we'd done was make an already sad girl absolutely miserable.

I knew God was not happy about this. He couldn't be happy when even one of His children is miserable.

And right now He had three miserable children: Loretta, Abby, and me.

7

Feeling Guilty

I lay on my bed, dressed in my school clothes, with my hands over my stomach. I had a terrible stomachache, the worst I'd had in a long time. I'd hardly slept at all during the night. I felt horrible, but it wasn't just because of my stomach or because I hadn't slept.

We had done a terrible thing to Loretta. I was sure she was feeling even worse than I was.

It was all my fault, mine and Abby's.

Why did I let Abby talk me into starting that rumor in the first place?

I knew it was wrong. God said it was wrong to "bear false witness against your neighbor," and now I knew why. God's so much wiser than we are. He knows telling lies about other people—even if we think we might be doing them a favor—just might hurt them. And now, instead of sticking up for Loretta, I'd made her feel horrible.

There was a tap at my door and Emmy poked her head inside.

"Time to go to school," she said.

"I'm not going," I said.

"You're not?" She took a few steps into my room.

"No, I'm not," I said. "I just decided. I'm too sick. I have a stomachache."

"Okay," she said. "I'll walk by myself."

She left and I heard her walking downstairs.

I really didn't feel well enough to go to school. But I also didn't want to face anyone there. Especially Loretta. I didn't want to see her sad face and be reminded about how much we'd hurt her.

I knew what was coming next. In a few minutes I heard heavier footsteps climbing the stairs.

Another tap sounded at my door.

"Come in, Mom," I said.

"Hi, honey."

She moved quickly into my room and sat on the edge of my bed. She felt my forehead.

"You don't feel feverish," she said.

"I have a stomachache," I said.

"You ate breakfast," she said. "Did you eat too fast?"

"No," I said. "I didn't feel like eating breakfast before I ate it."

"That's too bad, honey," she said. "I think you're right to stay home today." She stood up. "I'll call the office and tell them I won't be coming in today."

"But, you don't have to stay home with me!" I said. Now I felt even more guilty. Mom would stay home feeling sorry for me and miss a day of work all because I'd been such a jerk to Loretta. "I'll be okay here by myself. I'll just stay in bed or watch TV."

"I think I should keep an eye on you," Mom said. "I'll go call the office." She left the room.

I spent most of the day in bed. Mom gave me a hot water bottle. It made my stomach feel a teeny bit better.

But I needed something that would make me feel better about myself. No hot water bottle could do that.

The day seemed to last forever. Nothing I did took my mind away from Loretta and how sad she must be. Not books, not TV, not anything. It was awful.

At 3:45, I heard Emmy's feet clomping up the stairs. I heard her go into her bedroom and close the door.

"Emmy?" I called out to her. She didn't answer.

Just then the phone rang. I got out of bed, went into Mom and Dad's room, and picked up the receiver.

"Hello?" I said.

"Hello," said a kid's voice. There were giggles in the background. "Is this Emily's house?"

"Yes," I said. "This is her sister. Do you want to talk to her?"

"No," the voice said to more giggles. "But tell her to say hi to *Wodnot* for us."

"Who?" I asked.

The phone was hung up.

"*Wodnot?*" I said.

I went to Emmy's room, and knocked on the door.

"Come in," Emmy's muffled voice said.

I opened the door and found Emmy lying on her bed with her face pushed into her pillow.

"Somebody just called you," I told her.

She didn't answer.

"I don't know who it was," I said.

"I do," she said, her face still in her pillow.

"Who?" I asked her.

"Allie and Brianne," she said. "And maybe Hannah."

"Well, whoever it was said to say hi to Wodnot," I said.

Emmy let out a sob.

"What's the matter?" I asked her. "Who's Wodnot?"

Emmy turned over and looked at me. Her eyes and nose were wet and red. She wiped her nose with the back of her hand.

"Wodnot is an alien," she said.

"An alien?" I said. "You mean, like from outer space?"

"Yeah," she said. Then she looked away from me. "I told Hannah and those girls a—a lie."

"About an alien?" I asked her.

Emmy nodded. "I told them I'd seen a UFO," she said. "They seemed really interested, so I told them that it was this ship from outer space."

"Wodnot is an alien from outer space?" I asked.

"Yeah," she said. "He's the captain of the ship."

"But why did you tell them such a crazy thing?" I said.

"Well," Emmy said, "I saw how popular Loretta got when you and Abby told everyone that she was related to Alison St. John!"

Oh, no!

"And so," Emmy said, "I thought maybe I could make some friends by telling them something exciting about me. I thought it might make them want to be my friends."

"But they didn't believe you?" I asked her.

"At first they kind of believed me," she said. "They really believed that I saw a UFO. But they kept asking about the UFO, and I thought I'd better make up some more stuff to tell them. But when I said the UFO landed and I met this little blue space guy, they started laughing." She stopped and swallowed hard. "I guess I shouldn't have told them those lies."

I sighed. "Well, Abby and I shouldn't have made up that story about Loretta, either."

"But, Loretta got popular!" Emmy said. "I saw those girls acting as if they liked her!"

"But it didn't last. In fact, the whole thing blew up in our faces. And now Loretta is upset, and I feel horrible about what Abby and I did." I played with a strand of Emmy's hair. "It was an awful thing for us to do," I said. "I guess friendship and lies don't mix."

Emmy put her hands under her head. "What do you think I should do?" she asked me. "Those girls hate me."

I didn't even have to think hard about it. I'd already decided what I should do before Emmy had come home. Emmy should do the same thing.

"I think you should talk to Hannah and the others," I said. "Tell them the truth. And I think I should apologize to Loretta for making up that rumor about her."

Emmy's eyes got big. "Really?" she said. She looked pretty worried. "That sounds hard."

I sighed. "It sure won't be easy, I can tell you that. But I've been thinking and praying. I've told God how sorry I am for hurting Loretta. I know He forgives me. But now I need to tell Loretta. And you need to tell your friends."

"Oh, boy," she said. "I don't know if I can do it. What if they laugh at me or get really mad and call me a liar?"

"You don't have to do any more than say you shouldn't have done it."

Emmy blew out a long breath, "I don't know."

"It's better than pretending that ridiculous story is true," I said. I couldn't help laughing a little. "Wodnot? Where did you come up with that name?"

Emmy smiled a tiny bit. "I made it up."

"Well, it's a good name for an alien," I said. "But I still think you should talk to those girls. And listen—you won't be doing it by yourself. Jesus will help you."

There was a long pause. "Okay," she said. Just then, she sat up abruptly. "Oh, I wanted to tell you—"

"What?" I said.

"I saw Loretta at school today," Emmy said. "She looked like she'd been crying. And her mother was there, too, I think. At least, there was a lady there with her."

"Oh, boy," I said. "See what those lies did to her?"

Emmy nodded.

"Where were they? I mean, Loretta and her mother?"

"They were going into the counselor's office," Emmy said.

I got up from Emmy's bed.

"Where're you going?" she asked me.

"To call Abby and tell her we've got to go over to Loretta's house and apologize," I said.

Emmy's eyes got big. "You're going to her *house?*"

"Sure," I said. "Why not?"

"Because maybe her mother will be there!" Emmy said. "She might yell at you! I'd be so scared!"

"I know," I said. "But I've got to get this off my chest."

I started for the door.

"What if Abby won't go?" Emmy asked.

"Then I'll just go by myself," I said.

"Wow," she said. "You're brave."

I smiled at her. "You know what?"

"What?" she asked.

"My stomach doesn't hurt any more."

"Really?"

"Yeah," I said. "I'm scared to death, but I guess I know Jesus is with me. At least my stomach doesn't hurt!"

"You want to *what?*" Abby said.

Abby's face had suddenly turned white when I told her what I thought we should do.

I'd walked over to her house after telling Mom I was feeling a lot better. Mom hadn't wanted me to leave, but I told her I had to go to Abby's and talk to her about school. That was technically true.

"I want to go over to Loretta's and tell her what we did," I said to Abby. We were standing right inside her front door. "And then I want to apologize to her and tell her we want to be her friend."

"*Are you nuts?*" she said. "We can't do that!"

"Why not?" I said.

"Well, well, because—" she said.

"Abby, Loretta is *miserable!*" I said, interrupting her. "Emmy said she and her mother were at school today. Emmy said Loretta had been crying. They were going into the counselor's office."

"But what if she throws us out?" Abby said.

"Then, at least we'll know we did the right thing," I said.

"I don't know if I can do it," Abby said.

"Then let me do the talking," I said. "You won't have to say anything."

"I won't?" she asked.

"No," I said. "I'll apologize for both of us."

"It'll be really embarrassing," Abby said.

"I know," I said.

"What if her mother is there?" Abby said.

"What if she is?" I said.

"What if she starts yelling at us?" Abby said, her forehead creased with a worried frown.

"It won't be any fun," I said. "But we'll survive."

"But I don't want to get yelled at!" said Abby. "I'd probably start crying or something."

I didn't say anything for a moment.

"How about this—why don't we just start being really nice to Loretta? We can invite her over. Then she'll know that we like her and want to be friends!"

I said, "You don't have to go. I'll go by myself if you don't want to go."

Abby took a step back and leaned against the stair banister.

"Thanks for not calling me a chicken," she said in a soft voice. "Or a scaredy-cat."

"I'm as scared as you are," I told her.

She let out a loud sigh. "Okay," she said. "I'll go with you."

"You will?"

"Yeah," she said. "But I sure am a chicken!"

I smiled. "So am I."

She clucked like a chicken and I smiled.

"Come on," she said. "Let's get this over with."

Into the Lions' Den

Maybe she's not home," Abby said.

"We won't know until we knock on the door," I said.

We stood across the street from Loretta's house. I was so scared, my legs were shaking. I knew we were doing the right thing, but I'd never been so nervous in my life!

"Maybe her mother took her out for a milk-shake or something," Abby said. "That's what my mom does when I feel sad about something."

"Maybe," I said. "But we still won't know until we go over there and knock on the door."

"Yeah, I suppose," Abby said.

"You ready?" I asked her.

"No, are you?" she said.

"No. But I don't know if I'll ever be ready to talk to Loretta. So I think we should just *do* it."

"Yeah, I suppose," she said again. But she didn't sound as if she meant it.

"Okay," I said. "Let's go."

"Wait," she said, grabbing my arm. "What are you going to say?"

"I'm going to tell her what we did," I said. "And then I'll apologize."

"What if she starts screaming at us?" Abby asked. "Don't you think we should figure out what we'd do then?"

"If we figured out every single thing that could happen," I said, "we'll never go over and knock on the door."

"I s'ppose not," Abby said. "You're *sure* you really want to do this?"

"We have to," I said. "It's the right thing to do. Even if Loretta hates us for the rest of her life, she'll know who did it. She won't think the whole school is against her. She'll know it was just us and that we're sorry."

"Yeah," she said. "I guess."

"Come on," I said. "Let's get it over with."

"Okay," Abby said.

Before she could change her mind, I stepped off the curb and walked across the street. She caught up with me at the other side.

We walked up the front walk and up the porch steps. We stopped right in front of the door.

I knocked.

We waited.

"My heart is beating so hard!" Abby said, "I'm afraid Loretta will hear it."

"She won't," I said.

"How do you know?" she asked me. "Can't *you* hear my heart beating?"

"No," I said. "I can't hear it. My own heart is drowning it out."

"Now I know what Daniel felt like in the lions' den," Abby said.

"Yeah," I said. "I know what you mean."

Just then, the heavy door opened. A tall, thin lady stood there. She frowned when she saw us.

My mouth was dry, and for a second I thought it might not work.

But I managed to say, "Hello."

"Hello," she said. "What do you girls want?"

"Um, I'm Samantha Crowley," I told her. "Is this where Loretta Smeed lives?"

The lady's eyes narrowed. "Yes," she said in a very short, crisp voice that wasn't at all friendly. "What do you want?"

I swallowed. "Well, Mrs. Smeed," I said, "my name is Samantha Crowley and this is Abby Hart. Could we please talk to Loretta for a few minutes?"

Mrs. Smeed seemed to think for a couple of seconds about what I'd just asked her. At first I didn't think she would let us inside. Then she stood back and opened the door wider.

"Come in," she said.

She still didn't sound or look friendly.

Abby and I stepped inside.

"Sit down," Mrs. Smeed said. She pointed toward the living room.

I looked at Abby, then walked over to the couch and sat down. Abby followed me.

"I'll tell Loretta you're here," she said.

"Thank you," I almost whispered.

Now that I was inside Loretta's house again, I got even more scared. There was no escape now. I'd told Loretta's mother who we were. Loretta would know we'd been there.

I looked at Abby and she stared back at me looking terrified.

"The lions' den," Abby whispered. I nodded.

Please, God, I prayed, please help me do this. I'm really, really scared. Don't let Loretta scream at me or hit me or anything. I know I deserve it, but don't let her do it. Okay?

It seemed that Abby and I waited for a long time, but it might have been only a minute or two. I kind of lost track of time as I sat there sweating and praying.

Finally, I heard footsteps descend the stairs. I looked up at the doorway.

Loretta stood there with Mrs. Smeed behind her.

I stood up, feeling my knees tremble. "Hi, Loretta," I said.

Abby followed my lead and stood up too.

"Hi, Loretta," she said.

"Hi," Loretta said. Her eyes were red, and she glanced back and forth between Abby and me.

Mrs. Smeed still stood there. I wished she'd go and leave us alone.

"Could we talk to you for a minute?" I said.

Loretta took another step into the living room.

"Okay," she said.

She perched on the arm of the closest chair, and her mother stood next to her.

Why couldn't Mrs. Smeed just go away!

I sat back down and so did Abby. We couldn't relax, though, so we sat on the edge of the couch.

"Uh," I started out, "Abby and I wanted to talk to you, Loretta. We have something to tell you that's kind of hard to say."

"Yeah?" she said. Her face looked hard as if she was telling herself not to cry in front of us. "What about?"

"Well—" I said, "we—Abby and I—well, we" There was a silence while Loretta waited.

"I don't really know how to—"

Loretta waited.

"We—"

I looked at Loretta's eyes. In her eyes, I saw sadness and hope and dread all at the same time.

Tell her! a voice said inside my head.

"We did a terrible thing," I said to her.

Loretta didn't say anything. She sat there as if she were made of stone.

"We—we wanted to do an experiment," I said.

"What experiment?" she asked.

"We called it our 'Good Changes Experiment,' " I said. "But that was a stupid name. We were just trying to make ourselves feel good about doing something awful."

"What'd you do?" Loretta asked.

"We—we started a rumor," I said. "Just because we wanted to see how it would change."

"What do you mean?" she asked.

"You know how people change what they hear?" I said. "Have you ever played the Telephone Game?"

"Oh," Loretta said. "Yeah."

"Well," I said, "we thought it would be interesting to start a rumor and then see all the changes that the rumor took."

Loretta sat there and stared at me. Her mother put a hand on her shoulder. I couldn't tell what either of them was thinking. Their faces had no expression.

Abby spoke up. "We didn't mean to hurt anybody!"

"No, we didn't," I said. "We thought, if anything, maybe the rumor would make some nice changes in your life."

"So you told everybody that Mom—" she looked up at her mother, "was really my aunt. And that Alison St. John was my mother who ran away to Hollywood."

"No," I said, "you've got to believe me. We didn't say all of that! We just said that you were *related* to Alison St. John!"

"Oh, that's *all* you said!" Mrs. Smeed's face turned bright red and she glared at Abby and me. "You thought it would be *fun* to play a game with my daughter's life!"

"We're really sorry, Mrs. Smeed," I said. "We didn't mean to hurt—"

"Well, you *did* hurt Loretta!" Mrs. Smeed said. "You hurt her very much. And you hurt me too!"

This was terrible. I knew that Abby and I deserved what we were getting, but it sure wasn't easy to sit there and listen to Mrs. Smeed yell at us. All I could do was apologize.

"I'm sorry," I said again in a soft voice.

"Well, you *should* be!" said Mrs. Smeed loudly. "I hope you've learned your lesson!"

"We have," I said. I looked over at Abby.

"Yes, we sure have," Abby said. "We'll never, ever do anything like that again."

"I think you girls owe Loretta a public apology," said Mrs. Smeed.

"What do you mean?" I asked her.

"I want you to go to school and stand up in front of each of the fifth grades and tell the children what you did," said Mrs. Smeed. "Then you'll tell Loretta how sorry you are. I want to be sure that the children know where that dreadful rumor came from."

I looked at Abby. Her eyes were wide and scared. I was scared, too, but there was nothing else we could do.

"Okay," I whispered, looking at the floor. "We'll do it."

Abby looked at me, terrified.

"In front of all of the fifth-graders?" she said in a little voice.

"Wait," said Loretta. "You don't have to do that."

Her mother looked at Loretta, surprised.

"But you cried for nearly two days!" Mrs. Smeed said.

"I know," Loretta said. "But I think we should just forget it."

Abby and I looked at each other and back at Loretta.

"I know you're sorry for what you did," Loretta said. "You don't have to stand up in front of everybody and tell them you started the rumor."

"Thank you, Loretta," I said. The words came out in a rush. I was so relieved!

"But how about telling the kids around on the playground that the rumor isn't true?" Loretta said.

"Sure!" Abby and I said. "We'll tell everybody!"

"Well, I think the girls' parents should be told," Mrs. Smeed said.

I gasped. Having my parents mad at me would be worse than confessing what I'd done in front of sixty fifth-graders!

"No," said Loretta. "I think we should just forget it."

"Is that *really* what you want?" Mrs. Smeed asked her. "Are you sure?"

"Yes," Loretta said.

Mrs. Smeed shrugged. "Okay," she said, "if that's what you want, dear."

I got up and went to Loretta and gave her a hug. "You're a really great person, Loretta," I said. "I mean it."

Loretta smiled then, and it was wonderful. Her whole face warmed up, and for the first time since I'd met her, she really, truly looked *happy*.

Even her mother's face softened a little. She leaned over and gave Loretta a hug too.

Just as we'd promised, Abby and I went to school the next day and told all the kids that the rumor about Loretta wasn't true.

Loretta was really, really nice to tell us that we didn't have to tell them everything up in front of the classes. But Abby and I decided we should tell everybody that the whole thing was our fault. Not in front of each classroom but outside on the playground.

That didn't seem so scary.

So the next day when we got to school, we looked for Loretta. We found her standing next to the building in the sunshine.

"Come with us, Loretta," I called to her.

She smiled shyly and walked over to us.

"We're going to tell everybody the truth," Abby said.

"Yeah," I said. "You come too."

She hesitated a moment. "Okay," she said.

The three of us walked around the side of the building.

"Look," I said. "There's Hilary and Heidi."

They were standing with Brandi and Colleen on the USA map.

"Hi," Abby and I said after we'd walked over to them.

"Hi," Brandi said.

The girls all stared at Loretta.

"We have something to tell you," Abby said and turned to me.

"Yeah," I said. "All that stuff you heard about Loretta? Well, it wasn't true."

"We made it up," Abby said.

"You made it up?" Colleen said.

"We made up a rumor," I said, "that Loretta was related to Alison St. John."

"It was a lie," Abby said.

"Then everyone added to it," I said.

I held up my Official Scientific Notebook. "We wrote it all down in here," I said. "We wrote about how the rumor changed."

"So," Hilary said slowly, "all that stuff about Loretta wasn't true?" She asked us the question, but stared at Loretta while she asked.

"That's right," I said.

"I live with my real mother," Loretta said. "I'm not related to Alison St. John. I don't even know her!" She smiled a little.

"But I wish I did."

The girls laughed.

"Me too!" Colleen said.

"Wouldn't it be fun to meet her sometime?" said Heidi.

"Yeah!" everyone said.

Hilary turned to Abby and me. "Well, all I can say is, I hope you guys don't start a rumor about *me*!"

"Don't worry," I said.

"We'll never do that again in our whole lives!" Abby said.

"I can't believe how the rumor changed," Colleen said. "All you said was that Loretta was *related* to Alison St. John?"

"Yup," Abby said. "You guys did the rest."

"*We* changed it?" Hilary said. "*I* didn't change anything I heard!"

Abby opened her mouth to argue, but she looked at me, and I shook my head. What difference did it make who changed the rumor? We were to blame, anyway, for starting the whole thing in the first place.

We didn't have to tell many more people after that. As Abby had told me before, if you tell the two H's, it gets around fast.

After school, I met my sister at her classroom door. She had been really scared about coming to school and telling the kids she'd lied about the little blue space guy.

When her teacher dismissed the class, Emmy hung her head and walked toward the classroom door. Most of the kids ran out into the hall, almost knocking me over.

"Hey, Emily!"

It was Hannah. She called to my sister.

Emmy, who was in the middle of the room, turned to Hannah.

Hannah walked up to Emmy and started talking to her. I couldn't hear what they were saying, but Hannah smiled. Then Emmy smiled.

Then Emmy grinned from ear to ear and nodded.

They both started walking toward the door.

"Oh, hi, Samantha!" Emmy said when she saw me.

"Hi," I said to her.

"I'm going over to Hannah's house for awhile," Emmy said. "Is that okay?"

"That's just great," I said.

Emmy threw her arms around me and hugged hard.

"Thanks," she whispered.

I knew she was thanking me for telling her to be truthful with the kids. Everything had worked out.

"You bet," I said, hugging her back. "See you at home later."

It's funny how we learn lessons about how God wants us to live. I mean, our Sunday school teacher can tell us things, like not to bear false witness against our neighbor. But when we see for ourselves how badly someone can get hurt, we learn the lesson a lot better. But it's a lousy way to learn it.

I ended up telling my parents about it too. That wasn't much fun either. But it was good to get it over with.

I wish I hadn't hurt Loretta. I wouldn't hurt her for anything. In fact, Loretta and Abby and I all became best friends after Abby and I apologized.

It took awhile for Loretta's mother to be nice to us, but she must have finally forgiven us. About three months later, around Christmastime, Mrs. Smeed brought a big box of candy and cookies to Abby's and my families that she had baked, herself.

I sure am glad Loretta was so forgiving. I don't know if I would have forgiven so easily if someone had started a rumor about me. God forgives us easily. But what Jesus had to do to win that forgiveness wasn't so easy. He died on the cross to pay the price for the wrong things that we do.

I learned my lesson the hard way. I'll *never* start a rumor about anyone ever again. In fact, I won't even pass along a rumor I hear about someone else. It might not be true!

Every time I look at Loretta, I think how glad I am to have such a forgiving friend. Then I thank God for her forgiveness.

And then I thank Him for forgiving me too. Because that's where forgiveness comes from. From God.

He forgave us first, so that we can forgive one another.